The Curse of the School Rabbit

Judith Kerr

HarperCollins *Children's Books*

First published in Great Britain by
HarperCollins *Children's Books* in 2019
First published in this edition by HarperCollins *Children's Books* in 2020
HarperCollins *Children's Books* is a division of HarperCollins*Publishers* Ltd,
HarperCollins Publishers
1 London Bridge Street
London SE1 9GF

The HarperCollins website address is:
www.harpercollins.co.uk
1

ISBN 978–0–00–837756–4

Printed and bound in England by
CPI Group (UK) Ltd, Croydon, CR0 4YY

MIX
Paper from
responsible sources
FSC™ C007454

This book is produced from independently certified FSC™ paper
to ensure responsible forest management.

For more information visit: www.harpercollins.co.uk/green

To my grandchildren,
Alexander and Tatiana,
with all my love

It was all the fault of the school rabbit.

The school rabbit is called Snowflake, and it belongs to Miss Bennet who teaches the First Grade. If Miss Bennet didn't have Snowflake, she wouldn't be able to teach the First Grade or anyone else. They write stories about Snowflake for English and draw Snowflake in Art, and for Arithmetic they weigh Snowflake and measure Snowflake in both centimeters and inches.

I never liked Snowflake because when I was in Miss Bennet's class and trying to measure Snowflake's length in centimeters, Snowflake peed on me. Miss Bennet said it was an accident, but I think Snowflake did it on purpose.

Now my little sister Angie is in Miss Bennet's class, and she thinks both Snowflake and Miss Bennet are wonderful. Angie does all the story-writing and drawing and measuring of Snowflake, and she has even invented a Snowflake dance with which she shows off to the grown-ups. Actually Angie shows off a lot of the time anyway, and sometimes people say she takes after our father, who is an actor. But Dad always says that acting is not showing off but immersing yourself in the character. I don't think Angie immerses herself in a rabbit.

Having a father who is an actor can be either a good or a bad thing. It's good when people have seen him on television and say nice things about him.

It's not so good when he is out of work or "resting," as they call it, and he wanders around the house looking sad, and we can't have new clothes or vacations.

Dad had been having one of these "resting" patches for a while, and I was getting a bit worried because it was coming up to Christmas and I really need a new bicycle.

But then one evening Uncle Mike appeared unexpectedly while we were having our supper. We all like Uncle Mike. He and Dad were at acting

school together, but Uncle Mike didn't become an actor. He became a director, which is someone who gives actors jobs, so I was extra pleased to see him.

Uncle Mike was very excited. He said he had been asked to direct a film starring an actor called Gordon Strong, who used once to be famous. In the film Gordon Strong would play a dashing secret agent,

which is what he always used to do, but he would also have a partner. The partner would, of course, be less dashing, but it was work and the money was good, and it was up to Dad what he made of the part, said Uncle Mike.

Dad said, "Oh Lord! Gordon Strong!" and Uncle Mike said, "I know, but he's much better these days. In fact, I thought I might bring him around here. The family atmosphere, you know. He's very sentimental about families, never having achieved one himself."

Mom said, "Well, he'll be very welcome, of course," and Angie said (as I knew she would), "I'll do my Snowflake dance for him," but Mom said, "No, if Mr. Strong comes to see us, he and Daddy will just want to talk."

Then Dad said, "He won't like me being taller than him," and Uncle Mike said, "Well, most people are taller than Gordon Strong, but it might be a good idea for you to crouch down a bit, so that it won't be so noticeable." Then they all said the usual stuff about Angie and me being very polite to Gordon Strong, which we would have been anyway, and in the end Uncle Mike said he would bring him over the next day.

The next day when I came home from school, Uncle Mike and Gordon Strong had already arrived and they were talking with Dad in the living room. Dad was leaning forward in a way he doesn't usually do, so his head and Gordon Strong's head were more or less on a level because Gordon Strong was really quite short.

Uncle Mike said, "Tommy, say hello to Mr. Strong," and I said, "Hello, Mr. Strong," and Mr. Strong said, "Well hello, Tomasso," which I think is Italian.

There was a special snack waiting on the table with little sandwiches and cupcakes and I wondered when

we were going to eat it, but Uncle Mike and Dad and Mr. Strong kept on talking and Dad was looking very cheerful, so that was good. Mom said that Angie was supposed to be dropped off by someone and they were late, but just then the doorbell rang. I could hear Mom's voice in the hall, and Angie's, and someone else's, which seemed to go on rather. Then there was a sort of thump, and then the door flew open and Angie just stood there. She was holding something in her arms and she shouted, "Traraa!" like someone in the circus and then she threw out her arms and the thing jumped across the room, and it was Snowflake.

Dad said, "Angie, what on earth…?" and then the front door banged and Mom came in and said, "It was Miss Bennet, she was in a terrible state…" and Angie said, "We've got to look after Snowflake because poor Miss Bennet's mother is ill and Miss Bennet has to go and look after her, and I told her you wouldn't mind and she's given me a list of all the things Snowflake likes to eat."

Uncle Mike laughed, but I could see he didn't really think it was funny, and he said, "Well, Gordon, there you see it, ha-ha, that's family life." But Mr. Strong didn't say anything. He was standing absolutely still and looking down at Snowflake, who was peeing on his pant leg.

I'm not quite sure what happened next. I think Dad made a sort of lunge at Snowflake, but he must have tripped, and he and Mr. Strong both fell over. Mr. Strong was left half kneeling on the floor, but Dad was stretched right out on his stomach, reaching out for Snowflake, who'd got away, of course, and I saw Mr. Strong looking down at Dad and sort of measuring him. It was a bit like measuring Snowflake, only he was doing it in his head and frowning.

Uncle Mike helped Mr. Strong up and Dad got up too and everybody was apologizing and fussing about Mr. Strong's pants. They were pale gray but almost black where Snowflake had peed on them, and I think

they were beginning to smell a bit too. Uncle Mike was still trying to pretend that it was funny, but it wasn't a bit convincing.

At last Uncle Mike said in his pretend-jolly voice, "Well, after all this I think we deserve a snack," but Mr. Strong said it had been delightful meeting us all, but now he must go.

Mom said, "Won't you just stay for a quick drink?" and Mr. Strong said, no he was sorry, and Uncle Mike said, "Then let me drive you," and Mr. Strong said, "Thank you, but my driver is outside. I'll be in touch." And then he had to push past Angie who had gotten hold of Snowflake and was standing in his way by the door, and he gave a sort of shudder and left.

After this nobody said anything for a bit. We heard Mr. Strong's car drive off, and then Dad said, "Well, that's that."

Uncle Mike said, "It probably wouldn't have worked anyway. You're a good three inches taller than him and he spotted it, of course. Mind you, being peed on by a rabbit didn't help."

Angie said, "It wasn't Snowflake's fault. Mr. Strong was staring at it. Snowflake hates being stared at." Then she made a soppy face and said, "Poor bunny."

I looked at Mom, and I could see that, like me, she was thinking that now there wouldn't be much money for Christmas presents. I wouldn't have minded so

much, only I really, really need that bicycle. The
one I've got is about six sizes too small for me. So I
shouted at Angie. I shouted, "Poor bunny! Ha! I spit
on it," which is what the villain in one of Mr. Strong's
old movies always said, and Angie screamed, "Mom!
Tommy said he'd spit on Snowflake!"

Mom said, "Oh, stop it, both of you," and then
she said, "I think we all need some food inside us." So
we sat down at the table and we ate every bit of Mr.
Strong's special snack, and it was delicious but a bit sad.

Miss Bennet had brought a hutch for Snowflake to live in, and after we ate, Dad put it in the yard with Snowflake inside it. Then he and Mom read Miss Bennet's list of how to look after Snowflake, which was about three pages of very untidy handwriting, like they always tell us at school not to do, and Dad said, "OK, basically it's just two feedings a day and a weekly clean-out. But it seems that rabbits need exercise as well. Do you suppose they go to the gym?" Dad can be really quite funny sometimes.

Anyway, it made Mom laugh a bit and she said, "We could just let it run around in the yard," but Dad said there was a hole in the fence and it would get out. Then Mom looked at the list again and said, "She says to make it some sort of a harness and take it for walks in the park," and then they both looked at me, and I said, "No! I'm NOT taking that rabbit for walks in

the park," and Angie shouted, "I will! I will! I'll take Snowflake for walks," but of course she's too small, and in the end I had to say I'd do it because Mom and Dad would both be too busy.

This was because Mom was trying to become a teacher and they made her write a lot of essays and things, and Dad had to go to auditions, which are places where they give actors jobs. Anyway, Dad said I'd be the official rabbit keeper and I'd get paid 50p a day, which is £3.50 a week and more than my pocket money. And the way things were going, I thought I might have to pay for a new bike myself, so I'd better start saving my money.

The next day, which was Saturday, Mom and I looked at Miss Bennet's list together, and it said that Snowflake's harness should be made of a bandage, which wouldn't hurt Snowflake's skin, and Mom told me to go and buy one from the pharmacy.

The pharmacy lady is a bit fussy, and when I said I wanted a bandage, she said, "What sort of bandage?" and I wasn't sure, so I said what Mom sometimes says when she is trying to buy us clothes. I said, "Well, obviously nothing too vastly expensive."

The pharmacy lady looked a bit surprised and said, "None of our bandages are expensive, but I need to know what this bandage is to be used for." So then I had to say, "It's to make a harness for a rabbit." There were a lot of other people in the shop and I knew they'd laugh, and they all did, and I felt a total idiot.

When I got home, Mom wound the bandage around Snowflake's chest and tummy and tied it in a knot, with one of the ends left long for me to hold like a leash. Then we tried walking round the yard with it, and Snowflake was hopping around and seemed quite pleased.

"There, you'll have no trouble with giving this rabbit a little walk in the park," said Mom, and it did seem quite easy. The park is at the end of our street. It's really just a big rough patch of grass and bushes and a few trees. Nobody much goes there because there is a much nicer park not far away.

It poured with rain all Sunday, but on Monday I got up extra early to take Snowflake out before school. It was still quite dark, and there was nobody else

around in the park. Snowflake hopped around all over the grass and I held on tight to the end of the bandage until Snowflake finally stopped and sniffed at what looked like a small gap under a bush.

I said, "Don't be silly, Snowflake—that's not a rabbit hole," because there are no rabbits in the park and never have been. But Snowflake went on sniffing, and I was getting a bit bored, and then, suddenly, something came running and leaping

at us, and it was not a rabbit but a big black dog.
The dog was growling and barking and baring its teeth
and Snowflake did a great bound and clung to my
legs with all its horrible claws,
which hurt. But obviously
I didn't want the dog

to eat Snowflake. So I snatched Snowflake up to my chest and shouted at the dog to get away. But suddenly there was not just one dog but several, all different kinds and colors, and all barking like crazy, and I thought, *Perhaps they're going to eat ME.*

Only then, luckily, there was a whistle. It was very loud, and the dogs looked sort of embarrassed and stopped barking, and a quite small old lady appeared. She had wild white hair and a fierce expression and she was wearing a jacket with "Approved dog walker" printed on it. She blew her whistle again, and then she shouted at the dogs with words that Dad had told me were quite rude, and I saw that the dogs were all on

leashes, but they were those retractable ones, and the old lady just hauled the dogs right back toward her and made them sit down. She came and peered at Snowflake and said, "Ha! You were very nearly rabbit pie," and she turned to me and said, "Better take it home quick." Then she shouted, "All right, come along, you!" and blew her whistle and the dogs all jumped up again and then she and the dogs sort of melted away into the dark.

When I got home, I told Mom what had happened and how I'd saved Snowflake from the dogs, and I thought Snowflake would be grateful. But it just scarpered back into its hutch, and Mom said, "What's that smell?" and I found that Snowflake had peed on me. So I had to have a wash and all clean clothes, and in the end I was late for school, and I thought, *I hate that rabbit!*

Mom said that taking Snowflake for walks was
clearly a bad idea, and that Dad would mend the hole
in the fence, so that Snowflake could be let loose
in the yard. Mending stuff is not Dad's best thing,

but he did it anyway, though the patch in the fence
looked a bit rough. So then all I had to do was to feed
Snowflake and clean its hutch.

Dad was fed up because he'd auditioned for a part on television that he'd almost gotten, but then they gave it to someone else after all. It wasn't even a very good part, but, as Mom said, it would have helped to pay the bills. They were talking about it with Uncle Mike, who had come over to tell us that the film with Gordon Strong had been cancelled.

Uncle Mike said that there had been a big argument with the producer because Gordon Strong had

threatened to sue the film company for allowing him to be peed on by a rabbit, which was clearly crazy, and the producer had said he wasn't going to waste his money on making a film with a madman, and so now the whole thing was off.

"So where does that leave you?" said Dad.

Uncle Mike said, "Out of work," and Mom said, "Join the club," and they all laughed the way people do when they don't really think something is funny, and

I knew that it was no use even thinking about a new bicycle.

Mom had had an email from Miss Bennet to say that her mother was better, but still needed her, so would we mind looking after Snowflake for another few days? She'd also sent some money for anything Snowflake might need, and I thought Snowflake certainly needed me to look after it, so at least my rabbit-keeper's fee would be safe.

The only person in our house who was happy was Angie who sang, "Snowflake is staying, Snowflake is staying!" while doing her rabbit dance, until she began to splutter and cough, and Mom said, "You're not getting a cold, are you?"

She took Angie's temperature and it was quite high, and Angie had to go to bed. But this made her even happier because she wouldn't have to go to school in the morning and would be able to look out of her window and watch Snowflake in the yard.

Only, being Angie, she did rather more.

The way it usually worked was that Mom let

Snowflake out to scamper in the yard about
lunchtime, and then, when I came home from school,
I would retrieve Snowflake, put it back in its hutch,
and give it its rabbit supper. But the next day when I
went out into the yard after school, there was no rabbit.
It was quite cold and trying to snow, and I thought

perhaps Snowflake had managed to get back into the hutch, but it wasn't there either. So I shouted, "Mom!" But Mom said she'd left Snowflake hopping around in the grass as usual.

Then we both noticed one of Angie's slippers on the ground and Mom said, "Oh, no!"

When Mom opened the door to Angie's room, Angie's bed was empty, but I could hear her saying in one of her silly pretend voices, "Can I offer you one of these delicious cupcakes?" and there she was on the floor, in her nightie, having a tea party with her dolls. And then I saw that one of the dolls wasn't a doll at all; it was Snowflake. The reason I had thought it was a doll was that Angie had dressed Snowflake in some of the dolls' clothes. She'd tied a sort of bonnet around Snowflake's head, only Snowflake's ears got in the way, and she'd tried to put a doll's dress on it, which was much too small, but it didn't seem to bother Snowflake. All Snowflake wanted to do was to eat some special rabbit treats that Angie was feeding it.

Mom said, "Angie, you should be in bed," and went to pick her up, and then she said, "For goodness' sake, you're frozen! Whatever have you been doing?" and Angie said, "Snowflake was all alone in the yard, so I went out to see it, and we had a game of chase and we ran round and round,

and in the end I caught it, and now we're having a party because Snowflake likes parties…"

But then she started to cough a lot, and Mom said, "We'd better get you warmed up. I just hope this hasn't sent your temperature shooting up again."

I thought I'd better get the dolls' clothes off Snowflake

and put it back in its hutch. It didn't seem to mind either way; it just wanted to go on eating the special rabbit treats. I don't think Snowflake was as happy about parties as Angie said.

When Dad came home, I told him about Snowflake and the dolls' clothes, and he laughed a bit, but then he said, "Angie getting sick is all we need." He'd been to see his agent, who is a sort of friend to actors who tries to get them work, but the agent had only suggested something that Dad thought was silly, and at supper with Uncle Mike they talked a lot about the Profession being a dead end and perhaps one should get a normal job, which they do every so often, and it was very boring, so I went to bed.

I half woke up once in the night. I thought I heard Mom and Dad move around and Angie crying, but I went back to sleep. But in the morning when I got up Mom and Dad were only half dressed and Mom was checking her phone so that she could call the doctor. Only she thought he might not be in yet, and Dad was saying, "Well, try him, anyway," and Angie was crying again.

I said, "What's the matter with Angie?" and
Dad said that her temperature was sky high and
they needed the doctor to give her something for
it, and Mom said, "Just get yourself some cereal or
something, will you, Tommy," and went back to

prodding her phone. So I made myself some egg and bacon, which we normally only have on Sundays, and while the toast was on I went to see Angie.

She seemed to be asleep again, but her breathing was funny and her face was red and looked all wrong, and I worried a bit in case the doctor wouldn't know how to fix it. But then I thought, *They have all these new pills now that can fix anything.* And then I went to feed Snowflake, and I said, "It's all your fault, you stupid rabbit." And then I went off to school.

With all the fuss about Angie I'd forgotten that this was a special day at school because we were supposed to write a story that morning. It was for a competition. A big bookstore wanted children to write a story, and the best stories were going to win a prize, which was a lot of free books for their school, so our teachers were hoping we would win. The story had to be about an animal.

I had vaguely tried to think of a story about an animal, but then I'd forgotten all about it, so I was a bit stuck. But then I thought about Snowflake and how everything had gone wrong in our house since we'd had that rabbit dumped on us, and I also remembered an old film with Gordon Strong, where he was given a ruby ring that brought people bad luck. It was called *The Curse of the Ruby* and I thought I'd write a story called:

"THE CURSE OF THE RABBIT."

So I wrote quite a long story about a man who
was given a rabbit that was cursed, but the man didn't
know this, and the rabbit got bigger and bigger until it
was as big as a horse, and the man lost all his money,

so he could no longer afford new clothes or a car or even bus fares, so he had to ride to work on the rabbit, and the rabbit kept getting mixed up with the traffic, and the man kept getting parking tickets.

So he gave the rabbit to the zoo, which the rabbit preferred to getting mixed up with the traffic, and

the zookeeper knew how to undo the curse, and they all lived happily ever after, and I just had time to underline THE CURSE OF THE RABBIT when the bell went and they came to collect our papers. My teacher read it and said it was very imaginative.

When I got home from school, Mom said that the doctor had given Angie some stuff and she seemed a bit better, but then in the night she got sick again and the next morning the doctor came back to see her, even though it was Saturday.

I didn't hear what he said because Mom told me that it was time I cleaned out Snowflake's hutch, so I did, and I told Snowflake again that it was all its fault. But Snowflake just went around and around in the clean straw to make a nest for itself. So I shouted at it, "You are a curse!" and when I went back inside, the doctor was just leaving.

He said, "Look after your sister," as though I could, and Dad was scribbling down what the doctor said was an emergency number just in case.

Mom said, "I'll just take another look at Angie," and I went with her. Angie's face was no longer so red, but it was sort of shrunken and her breathing was still all wrong, and when Mom said, "Hello, Angie," she didn't seem to hear and didn't even open her eyes, and Mom held my hand very tight and said, "We'll get her through this, won't we?" and I said, "Yes," even though I had no idea how.

We usually all go out and do something nice on weekends, but I could see that with Angie sick we'd have to stay in and look after her, which was a bit sad. But just as I was trying to think what to do with myself, Uncle Mike appeared and said, "So, young Thomas, how would you like to come out with me for a film and a pizza?" I suppose Mom must have called him.

So I had a margherita pizza with extra mushrooms, which is my favorite, and then we saw a film about a bear that has all sorts of adventures, and I thought it would be a bit babyish, but actually it was really good, and Uncle Mike thought so too.

When we got home, Angie was asleep, and Mom and Dad were having an argument about Shakespeare. Mom was saying, "But you love Shakespeare," and

Dad said, "Yes, of course I love Shakespeare, but they wouldn't want me and, anyway, stage work just doesn't pay, and I'm not going to leave you on your own with Angie so ill."

Mom said, "I wouldn't be on my own—Tommy will be here," and then she said, "You'd always regret it if you didn't give it a try," and it turned out that the agent had told Dad to go to an audition at a big theater where they only do Shakespeare, and in the end Dad said, "All right, I'll go if you're sure you'll be OK."

So next morning Dad went off to the theater, and he didn't mind so much because Angie hadn't woken in the night—which seemed like a good sign—in fact she was still asleep—and Mom took one of her study books to sit in Angie's room for when she woke up. I went out in the yard to feed Snowflake. It was cold, but a lovely day and as I opened the hutch, Snowflake sneaked past my hand and leapt down into the grass.

I suppose it wanted to hop around in the
sunshine, so I said, "All right, you silly rabbit, if
that's what you want. I'll feed you later."

Then I went back into the kitchen and dumped the
breakfast things in the dishwasher, and I was just going
to ask Mom if there was anything else she wanted me

to do when the phone rang and it was Uncle Mike to ask after Angie. I heard Mom say, "She's still asleep." Then she said, "Why don't you come over for lunch? Then you can hear all about Shakespeare," and she asked me to go and sit with Angie while she sorted out some food.

So I went into Angie's room and sat down on Mom's chair by the bed. Angie was almost completely covered by the blankets, but what I could see of her face was less red and she was making less noise breathing. So I said, "Hi, Angie," but she didn't answer, only I somehow thought that she had heard me, so I thought I'd try saying something more interesting. I made my voice go quite deep and I said, "Rrrrrabbit, rabbit, rabbit!" and she still didn't say anything, but this time I knew she'd heard me because something in her face was different. So I went on saying rabbit in different voices until she opened her eyes just for a moment and said in a little tiny voice, "Rabbit?"

I said, "Good morning, rabbit. You've had a
big sleep," and Angie opened her eyes completely
and said, "Have I?" and I said, "It's nearly eleven
o'clock," and Angie said, "I was dreaming... Have I
missed breakfast?" and I said, "I don't think anyone
will mind," and just then Mom came in and so Angie
said, "Can I have a boiled egg with wheat toast and
butter?" and Mom's face went all pink and wide with
a huge smile and she said, "Of course you can."

So then the day became quite different because
Angie was better, and Mom let her get up just for the
dessert at lunch with Uncle Mike, and it all became
like a party. Dad was talking about the audition

and saying how wonderful it had been to hear
Shakespeare spoken by such brilliant actors, and,
even though the result had just been the usual, "We'll
be in touch," it had been worth it for the experience.

Uncle Mike was talking about the film we had
seen together and how both children and grown-
ups could enjoy it, and why couldn't they make a
film like that instead of that silly stuff with Gordon
Strong, until Mom said, "Goodness, it's almost

dinner time." And just then the telephone rang and it was Miss Bennet to say that her mother was all better and she'd come and collect Snowflake in the morning. And then I remembered that Snowflake had been loose in the yard without food all day long,

so I left them all talking and went quickly to feed it and put it back in its hutch.

It was quite foggy in the yard and at first, when I couldn't see Snowflake, I wasn't worried. I thought the silly rabbit must be hiding. But then I realized that it really wasn't there, and I thought, *What on earth…?*

And then I remembered Dad's patch on the fence, and I peered at it through the fog, and instead of the patch there was a hole big enough for a whole herd of rabbits to get through into the yard next door.

I still wasn't too worried because the hole was big enough for me to squeeze through, and I thought I'd just retrieve Snowflake and bring it back.

But Snowflake wasn't in that yard either, and then I saw that there was a little alleyway that led around the side of the house to the street.

So the stupid rabbit had got out. It could be anywhere. Anywhere at all. And it was all my fault for forgetting to feed it.

I thought, *This really is the Curse of the Rabbit.* I could just imagine Miss Bennet's face when she came the next morning and there was no Snowflake. And Mom and Dad would be angry. As for Angie... I thought, *I must find that rabbit.*

All the houses in our street have little front yards, and I thought that Snowflake would have gone into one of those. So I started walking along one

side of the road in the fog and peered into each
yard, to see if Snowflake was there, but there
was no sign of it. Then I walked back up the other
side. It took ages, and there was still no rabbit. So
that only left the park. I thought, *Surely Snowflake
would never go back there after all that fright with
the dogs.*

But I couldn't think of anywhere else to look, and
it was the only choice, other than going home and
telling everybody what had happened. So I thought I
might as well try it.

By this time the fog had
gotten even thicker,
and as I crept around
staring down into the
almost invisible grass
in the park, I wondered
whether I would be able
to see Snowflake even if
it was there. I was looking for

anything white, and once, for a moment, I thought
I'd found it, but it was only a plastic bag.

And then, suddenly, I heard a dog barking and
a voice shouting at it, and I thought, *Oh, no! Not
again!* There was a wobbly light from a flashlight
and a wrinkled face with wild white hair appeared
out of the fog, and of course it was the old lady dog
walker with just one small dog this time. I suppose
she was taking it home.

The light wavered all over
the ground, and I saw that we
were standing more or less
in the place where we
had met before, where
Snowflake thought
there was a rabbit
hole. I tried to tell
the old lady about
Snowflake escaping,
just in case she might
have seen it, but the

little dog kept barking and she kept shouting at it, and she just said, "Rabbits, eh?" and the little dog barked one more big bark—it had a really loud bark for such a small dog—and they went off into the fog.

And then, suddenly, something leapt at me out of the darkness and clung to me with all its horrible

scratchy claws, and it was Snowflake! And I was so pleased—so terribly, terribly pleased—that all I could think of saying was, "Oh, Snowflake…! Snowflake…!" And then I said, "Really, Snowflake, I told you that there are no rabbits in the park."

And I clutched Snowflake tight against my chest and wondered if it would pee on me again, but I thought I wouldn't mind even that too much, and we set off toward home.

As we got back to our street, I wondered if I need tell anyone about Snowflake's escape. After all, I was the official rabbit keeper, and it was really my fault.

Well, Dad's fault as well, because if he'd made a decent patch on the fence Snowflake couldn't have gotten out, only he might not see it that way. I wondered if Mom and Dad had missed me. I thought that with luck they might all just have gone on talking and I could feed Snowflake and then walk in as though nothing had happened.

So I was walking as fast as I could with my arms glued around Snowflake, and trying to watch where I put my feet because it was really getting hard to see, when someone came toward me out of the fog ahead, and it was Uncle Mike. I started to say, "Hello, Uncle Mike," but he just stared at me.

Then he said, "Boy with rabbit," and he stared at me some more through a shape he made with his fingers, which I know is what he does when he is thinking how to shoot a bit of film. Then he said, "Boy with rabbit in fog. Don't move, Tommy," and

he got out the little camera he always carries and took a whole lot of pictures. Then he put his arm around my shoulder and said, "I'll walk home with you," even though he'd clearly only just come from there.

When we got home, Dad opened the door, and I started to say, "Dad, Snowflake got out..." but Uncle Mike said, "Just put it back in its hutch, Tommy. Your father and I have to talk." Then he said, "Alfred," which is my father's name, "Alfred, I've got an idea."

So I put Snowflake back in its hutch and gave it an extra lot of food, and it hadn't peed on me, which was a relief. When I got back to the living room, Mom and Dad and Uncle Mike were all talking and interrupting each other, and then Dad said, "This calls for a drink," and they talked a lot more, and then Angie appeared in her nightie and Mom said, "You should be in bed," but then she wrapped Angie in a big blanket and let her stay.

It turned out that Uncle Mike wanted to make a different film instead of the one with Gordon Strong, and this film would be for children, but also for grown-ups, like the one about the bear he and I had seen together. Uncle Mike thought he could persuade the producer to do this, especially as he already had an idea of what the film should be about, and he knew the producer had the money. "A boy and a rabbit," said Uncle Mike. "Boy gets rabbit. Boy loses rabbit. Boy finds rabbit. That's basically what it always boils down to, and I know just the person to write it."

Then he said, "Tommy, how would you like to be a film star? Would you like to act the boy with the rabbit?" and I didn't know what to say. I like it when Dad is acting and I like watching people act in films and on the TV, but I've never thought about doing it myself. So I said, "I don't know," and then there was a sort of hoarse squeal from inside Angie's blanket

and she shouted, "I will! I will! I'll act the boy with the rabbit!" and everybody laughed, and Dad gave Angie a hug and said, "You'd act the BOY with a rabbit?" and Angie said quite loudly, "Yes. And why does it have to be a boy, anyway?" and Dad and Uncle Mike looked at each other and Uncle Mike said, "She's got a point."

Then I helped Mom put Angie back to bed and I told Mom a bit about Snowflake escaping, and she said, "Oh, well, carpentry was never your father's best thing," and I said, "I was a bit late feeding Snowflake," which was sort of true, and she said, "Better clean the hutch out before Miss Bennet comes tomorrow." So I did that, and the next day when I got home from school, both Snowflake and the hutch were gone. It was quite odd. I almost missed them.

But when I went into the house it was even odder. There in the living room were Dad and Uncle Mike, both looking rather dressed up, talking to a strange man, and there on the table was one of Mom's special snacks all laid out, and Uncle Mike said, "Tommy, come and say hello to the great Charlie Collins."

But Mr. Collins was not at all like Mr. Strong. He was tall and quite large and jolly, and he said, "Ah, so this is the rabbit keeper. I'm sorry I've missed meeting that rabbit. I wanted to shake it by the paw.

Any rabbit that pees on Gordon Strong's pants is my friend," which I thought was very funny.

Then Angie and I had our own special snack in the kitchen because, Mom said, Charlie Collins was the producer and he and Dad and Uncle Mike needed to talk. They were still talking when we'd finished eating, so we watched the little TV in the kitchen until bedtime, and I heard the front door go just as I was dropping off to sleep, so the producer must have stayed to supper as well.

The next morning, Dad was very cheerful, and I said, "Are they going to make the film about the rabbit?" and Dad said, "Well, you never know with films, but it looks as though they possibly might," and Mom said, "Anyway, how would you like to see your father playing Shakespeare in the theater?" and it turned out that when the theater people had said, "We'll be in touch," they had actually meant it and they had called to offer Dad a job. I hadn't realised that ever happened. Anyway, Dad kept talking about the wonderful actors he would be working with and he and Mom were smiling, and neither of them said anything about stage work being badly paid, so I suppose it didn't matter. Only I thought I'd better keep saving my money, just in case.

But then Uncle Mike and the producer kept coming around to our house to eat, and sometimes the lady who was writing the script came too, and Angie and I got to see a lot of television in the kitchen. Dad said it was because they all enjoyed Mom's special snacks so much, and they really had to make the film, just so that they could keep coming. But, anyway, now it's really going to happen, and Dad and Angie are both going to be in it. Angie is going to do her rabbit dance, because the producer said it would bring the house down, which I think means that people will like it.

My story about the Curse of the Rabbit didn't win a prize, but got a special mention for originality. But, actually, it's weird how everything went wrong in our family from the moment Snowflake arrived and peed on Gordon Strong. And how everything went right again as soon as Snowflake had gone. It really was as though Snowflake could put a curse on people. On the other hand, if Snowflake hadn't escaped and Uncle Mike hadn't met me in the fog, he might never have thought of the rabbit film. So it's a puzzle.

Anyway, now it is Christmas Eve and we are
having a party around the Christmas tree with
Uncle Mike and the producer and some
of the other film people, and Mom has
invited Miss Bennet as well, but without
Snowflake, and Miss Bennet is telling the
script lady all about rabbits.

There is a very special supper
with a big Christmas cake,
and there are candles
everywhere, and it
is all beautiful, and
Mom and Dad are
smiling, and
Angie and I are
thinking about
tomorrow…

... AND I GOT IT!

I got a new bike! It is blue and silver, and it has different speeds and bendy handlebars, and it is almost twice as big as my old one, and I am going to ride it and ride it, and ride it, till I am grown up!